LGBT Fiction

WITCH

Science Fiction Fantasy Short Story

by Rebecca Little

LGBT Fiction
WITCH
Science Fiction Fantasy Short Story
A story by Rebecca Little
Cover Art by Indie Artist Press
Published by Indie Artist Press
Eagle Mountain, Utah
www.indieartistpress.com
First Print Edition
copyright © 2013-2015
All rights reserved.
ISBN-13: 978-162522-030-1
March 2015

Witchwill soon become a feature length motion picture from The Oxford Comma Film Cooperative.

You can get in on the action by taking a looksee at the IndieGogo Campaign page here:

https://www.indiegogo.com/projects/witch-the-feature-film

Thanks for your support!

For Wade and Ama, with love.

A buzz.

My couch is gone. My fridge too. So are my rug, lamp, kitten and clothes. Everything. I don't fill much space in my purged apartment, 6 floors up from the first layer of concrete crust coating this city. It felt so small before, barely enough room for one person, but now far too naked to really be considered a home. There's a clue, barely left safety-pinned to a lingering curtain.

72. *That is all.*

Down six flights of stairs and out through double doors into a sun-showered morning. Door left unlocked. Of course, the key missing too. Alas.

I walk the six blocks to Erica's house. Still there. That sheepishly light blue shingled house with white trim. She always ends up in houses like these. When I used to go over to her house back in elementary school while her parents were at work, those same blue shingles, lined in white. We rarely kept to her house though. There was an abandoned house just down the block. We thought it was haunted because the inside burned out decades ago in an electrical fire. All that was left was the outer shell, standing stubbornly together, window trim still blackened from the fire within.

Erica thought spirits followed her home. I would shrug and puff on my pre-pubescent cigarette like I was the shit. She would have some answers, or at least a theory or two.

Erica lives alone. Not on purpose, but as a by-product of broken plans. Now she lives up a flight of rickety old stairs on top of the other half of a lovably crumbling house. She used to write feverishly. Mostly mysteries. She liked to put herself in the plot.

I knock on the door. She comes, draped in a shawl and panties. They're white and green striped. Erica likes underwear way more than pants.

She lets me in and pours two cups of lavender tea. "Calms the nerves," she says.

The funny thing is, I don't feel panicked at all. Not that big, solid things usually disappear into thin air, it just doesn't seem to make any difference. I tell her this.

"Maybe you're not worried because they were never solid to begin with," she suggests. "Maybe they disappeared because you're ready to see things as they are."

I shrug.

"You didn't come to me for help."

"Then what did I come for?" I ask.

Of course. Now I know. This is just the paranormally-charged world Erica craves come-true. I've brought her a gift. Our eyes meet in gratitude and I nod with a smile.

Erica picks up her cup of tea and takes a short steamy sip. "Read any good books lately?" she asks.

"Dr. Seuss," I grin. I've been baby-sitting a six-year-old named Aima. She likes to be read to, but she always tries to change the story around mid-plot. Sometimes I let her, but not with Seuss. He has too much good stuff to say.

"Dr. Seuss, huh?"

"Maybe Aima's the good book. She just gets it. All that stuff we talk about, she lives it. Reality being thin, life being made of things we see that probably aren't real and space where things that are real live but we can't see them. She just does it. She makes us into characters she thinks up in her mind."

We've been playing a very intense make-believe game. Aima's favorite. She calls it Witch, loosely based on Wizard of Oz, except she's a princess and I'm her unicorn. The witch chases us and tries to catch us and will probably do terrible, unspeakably evil things to us. We narrowly escape when Aima gives us new, very convenient powers at the last minute every time.

"We should play sometime," Erica smiles.

I shake my head.

One day, after we'd finished playing Witch, just before her bedtime, Aima told me the witch would never stop hunting us, that we would be playing this game forever. I knew this was just her tactic for holding my attention, thus obligating me to play with her in the future. But something about the certainty that being hunted by this begrudging witch figure would never end hit a bit too close to home.

"She's a smart one," Erica says. "She knows how to seal a deal."

"Even if everything I own disappears, I still have to play Witch with her tomorrow."

I drift off to sleep on Erica's couch, wondering whether my house and possessions will reappear in the morning or if this familiar space will vanish as well. I feel her slip away into spaces between words and sensations in the next room, her chaos mixing with my numbness. I suddenly live on Neptune with nothing.

By the end of the dream, I've acquired space friends and a moon boat. Now I'm awake on a spaceship.

They're not exactly how you'd expect aliens to look. Yeah, they have big heads, huge eyes and gray flaccid skin, but they have two sets of legs, and instead of arms they have ideas. These ideas constantly change color and intention and look like long spools of psychedelic thread. They are short. I am not afraid.

I don't even try to ask where I am or why. There's no point in demanding an explanation. I know Erica will wake up wondering where I am.

They have tables and chairs made out of long, woven idea threads, ever shifting, never solid, but somehow I can sit on them comfortably. I watch through a window as stars streak by in firework fan clubs, excited to catch a glimpse of a favorite asteroid.

"Stars aren't fanatic about asteroids," an alien comments, thinking about strawberries on Pluto in shades of turquoise and tangerine. "They don't dislike them though."

Why is that?

"They don't get along because when one touches the other, the same one always melts," the alien says, arms turning white and wispy. "For your intents and purposes, you may call me Arnold."

Arnold the alien with ideas for arms. I like him.

Reality is thin up here in space, when down and up and here and there are the same and opposite at once. There are no reference points, no set distances between unspecified and ever-shifting places. I become a triceratops for a bit, but just in my head and it weaves out in pointy, prehistoric threads where my arms used to be. Arnold laughs.

"It just takes some getting used to."

Where are we going?

"Have you ever been inside a black hole?" he asks.

No, not that I remember.

"Well, you probably won't remember this time either."

I watch out the window as we approach what looks to be space's vagina, a black hole amidst a hairy snatch of every-colored gases and strings of space follicles and ideas.   Arnold tells me to forget everything I believe about myself because none of that will help me where I'm about to go.   Universes—imaginable and beyond— suck sensually through this mysterious, dark gape. Wonder and peace float back. Space slurps.

Arnold holds my hand without lifting a finger.

I wake up on the bedroom floor of my own apartment, covered in my things. My kitten curls at my feet. I see my couch through the door leading to my living room and hear the buzz of my fridge in the kitchen. The digital clock beside my bed reads solidly nine AM. Time to brush my teeth and play with Aima.

The problem with reality being thin is it makes for very short stories. Characters never stay in one piece long enough to become real people. Settings squirm too often to describe and plot lines twist and turn like a shape-shifting inchworm in full orgasm.

Erica and I first realized this when she used to write stories. She'd get frustrated because she could never make them quite long enough.

"Other writers can drag scenes on for pages and write long-ass books with half the plot space as mine, but I just can't do it," she'd complain, thrusting a fifty-paged thriller into my arms and demanding an opinion. "The story's fucking over and it's far too short!"

Aima's mastered the art of lengthening a story amidst a shifting world. She firmly believes in the dichotomy of good and evil.

"Can't we just be nice to the witch, try to understand where she's coming from and try to convince her to be good?" I plead with her. I'm trying to develop the witch's character, discovering clues about her past and how she became so begrudging and miserable. Aima doesn't care.

"She's just evil and she hates us."

"But why?" I ask.

"Because she's a *witch*."

And I'm a unicorn.

Aima finds a set of magnetic letters to stick on a fridge and leave messages, half missing, in a broken piñata hung on a large pine tree. She says the *q* has special powers because it can also be a *p*, *b*, or *d*. "She won't be able to catch us for 30 seconds, so we can get away."

She'll catch up with us soon enough anyway.

I once described a nightmare to Aima in which these very pale women with arms outstretched all the way out to their sides hovered slowly towards me across the parking lot of a local mall in my hometown. I tried to escape, but it felt like running through sand and I could only move very slowly.

"That's what the witch looks like," she said.

I carry Aima on my back in circles around her back yard — one of those tasks I'd agreed to by default when I became her unicorn. Her short, curly blond hair tickles the back of my neck just above where her tiny hands clasp. "She's in the tree!" Aima squeals.

Sometimes, I fight back. "Witches can't climb trees," I argue.

"She flew, and she's really tall, so she

could just step into the tree anyway."

I want to argue back, but if she's so damn big, how come the branches don't snap under her weight. But I know Aima will reply, "Because she's light as a feather."

72 stickers

on Emma's binder in sixth grade. She sat next to me and never really said much. Emma had pens in all kinds of crazy colors and she'd switch off blue for green for pink for magenta for emphasis and back again, sometimes even within the same word.

72 eyelids

in the Greyhound station in Madison at midnight, surrounded by sleeping warehouses and snoring streets. I hear there's life developing on that Texas-sized plastic bag island floating out in the middle of bum-fuck nowhere Pacific Ocean. They're tiny, eat plastic, and believe in ghosts.

72 songs that remind me of my mom.

72 books read to completion in the past five years.

72 blankets in a summer camp.

72, that is all.

My things are not back. Not really. Whenever I go to brush my teeth, I pick up that same plump tube of toothpaste and nothing comes out. I eat leftover burrito from my fridge and no taste fills my mouth. No food travels down my throat into no digestive track. I go to take a shit and the damn toilet won't flush. Is the illusion of my life better than nothing at all?

I think about going back to Erica's house after playing with Aima. Part of me wants to tell Aima what happened, part of me knows she understands even if there's nothing she can do about it. Words well in my chest as I carry her on my back across the meadow to her favorite park. "My life isn't real anymore," screaming up through the top of my head because my lips are sealed tight.

Aima's favorite park is one of those

old wood-and-metal contraptions. It's simple and solid. She glides across the bridge as I lurk beneath pretending to be a troll. She doesn't like when I'm not on her side.

"The witch turned you evil," she says spitefully. "She turned me evil too, but we don't know it yet, but I'm telling you now so we're on the bad side, but we think it's good."

She wants to kill the fairies in the tree that had helped us escape earlier. She cackles like she means it. I wonder if she does. I'm not much in the mood for murdering fairies, I tell her. Aima pouts.

72 fairies at the ball. They're very small. They like to lounge in champagne glasses before cocktails are served. I almost choked on one once. She was pissed at first,

but now we laugh about it. Her name is Mirrribelle. Her voice is bubbles. They drift up into letters and colors and symbols, popping into sound and silence.

I end up at the fairy ball after leaving Aima. I didn't want to go back to my less-than-imaginary apartment (probably to find the door locked, no matter how many times I run the key through it). It feels like a fairy ball down here at the beach, just far enough down the train tracks and through the woods to spend a summer night naked. Malt liquor and mayhem.

Wood pallets burn like a supernova. Naked men and women dance and drink, some racing off into the lake, others into the woods. Colt 45 in brown paper bags and smoking joints float around the crowd. "It's been a while," Wade whispers, startling me as I stare into the fire.

He giggles as I leap and hug him in one very awkward movement. Wade used to live with me in an old house. There were three other tenants besides Wade and me. Wade didn't actually pay rent, but he work-traded carpentry. I can't wield a hammer for shit. We were all basket cases, but every one of us had a heart of gold.

A heart of gold is hard to carry.

Especially when it clangs against your ribcage when you dance and crushes your spine when you lie down to rest.

Wade's eyes glisten in the firelight. Wade's eyes would have glistened in a pitch black hole. His face, familiarly covered in smile lines stretched around sunken eyes with warm, happy lips. "How ya been, kid?"

"It's been doing," I reply.

"You feel different, what's a matter?"

I sit there with naked Wade, butts in the sand at water's edge, feet outstretched in cool waves. Wade passes his plastic-bottled vodka my way. Scrunching my nose, I pour it down my throat and it fills my chest with warmth. My shirt is somewhere. He rubs my back with one hand and reclaims his bottle with the other.

"Something happened and my home isn't real anymore."

Wade's used to my changed mind, changed plans, changed clothes three times a day but none of them are actually clean. He's used to my dilated pupils first thing in the after-morning-noon. I'm used to his strange cycles. I'm used to needles in his arm, I'm used to his broad gestures and splendid stories that probably didn't happen but are worth the while to listen to. I'm used to his back rubs and the way his hugs smell late at night. I'm used to his unapologetic laugh. I'm used to his moral high ground even when he's talking shit like an angry toilet.

"Well that could mean just about everything," Wade slurs.

"It does."

Wade smashes his bottle into the sand creating an instant cup-holder, cracks his neck and says, "Congratulations kid, you're entirely free."

A molten heart of gold.

With a gentle flick, Wade catches a tear rolling down my cheek, tangling his finger lovingly around a wisp of idea thread where my cheekbone used to be. He chuckles, leans in and kissed sandstorms out at sea, curling in pearly idea threads softly. They blush crimson and he tells me I'm beautiful.

Wade hoists himself up and swaggers into the black, space-lit lake and disappears beneath its still surface in a gentle dive. A minute. He's probably come up somewhere across the lake, in the darkness. Three, four, five minutes.

"Wade!" I call out across the lake.

I bolt up and crane my neck across the black crystal surface, scanning liquid constellations for any sign of a ripple, listening intently for a reply.

The circle around the fire bursts out in laughter. Not joyous laughter, but that manic laughter following a joke in bad taste.

"Happens a few times a summer, I reckon," a man wearing nothing but a blue speedo sighs, leaving the circle to place a warm hand on my shoulder. "Can't help it, though. I done it once or twice."

Wade?

"You haven't been here a while, have you?"

It's been a while, yeah.

"Wade drowned a while back," the man says.

My molten heart of gold drips down into my belly.

"He was drunk as usual, a bit more if you ask me," the man says, slurring with pain in his voice. "He went out for a swim, came up dead."

Reality is really thin here.

A buzz.

Same place, filled with fairies. 72 naked bodies dance around the fire. The trees in the forest surrounding us are green with thick, flat trunks and tiny little scrapings unraveling every few feet. Tall blades of grass in an impossibly large backyard. My favorite lake, but a puddle leftover from a relatively prehistoric storm. Delicate wings sprout from each back, some stained and torn, others look brand new. Some are even pierced and dipped in paint.

Some wings are coated in a light glaze of hair, like gentle beards.

What do my wings look like?

"That's the big mystery," says the fairy in the blue Speedo. "None of us have the words to describe another's wings, only you have the words for your wings. All I can do is look at 'em, and all you can do is wonder what it is you have the perfect words for. Funny trade off."

Indeed.

Fairy dust tastes like freshly cut grass in a cotton-candy Halloween costume.

Aima knows this. Here I am again, her little arms wrapped around my knees.

"Can we play Witch today?"

No, not today.

"Why not?"

I just don't feel like it.

The last thing I want to do right now is play that eternal game of lethal tag. I want to tell Aima I'm sick of playing a game with no end. I'm sick of being reduced to crafty prey. I'm sick of playing mouse.

I want to tell Aima there's no such thing as stagnant good and evil, but I know she'll just cross her arms and assert, "But the witch is evil, and we're good!"

So I say nothing and hoist the princess onto my unicorn back.

Sparkling fairy dust drifts up from the pulse of dancing bodies around the fire and floats out over the lake. My arms become sparkling streamers dancing off into wispy water and trickling down through surface tension and seaweed. Fairy dust becomes snow underwater. Aima knows this, even though she still won't accept things become different when their surroundings change.

Erica's naked body moves hypnotically, folds of fat in just the right places jiggle with each bounce. She dances with her arms, her legs, her hips, her eyes. Firelight glows off her hair and cheeks. I want to tell her how specifically beautiful her wings are, but I don't have the right words. I feel them formulate foggy near the roof of my mouth, then instantly fumble and fall apart.

Erica looks at me with lust and magic in her eyes. She lusts to give me words for what I will never know and she will never understand.

A buzz.

My petals are light and white. They feel like silk from within. I don't remember being a flower before.

"Flowers don't ever remember anything," scoffs a violet.

Then how come you remembered that?

"I used to be a music note," she explains. "Middle C to be exact. I drifted on a breeze from the bell of a trumpet, over the meadow and landed in the earth right here."

And then you grew into a violet.

"Exactly."

I was once E minor.

"How haunting of you."

I slurp up water from the spongy ground around my roots. Thirst quenched in my toes and moving up, the opposite of what I vaguely remember being used to. I flex my leaves and petals towards sunlight and she beams down on me through a thin layer of clouds. Earthworms wriggle nearby and their vibrations massage me.

"I saw you come down last night," says the violet.

How did I get here?

"I've felt it a few times before. There's a rumbling, low at first then it grows louder and louder and the ground is pelted with E minors. Rumors spread across pastures, plots and meadows about corn and soy and wheat and barley broken to form big shapes we can only feel through vibrations and loneliness."

A crop circle?

"What's a crop?"

A plant grown specifically to be eaten.

She weeps in middle C.

What you feel is a million and infinity worlds overlapping at once. A million and infinity points in time, in possibility, in imagination, in the spaces between, within and through. These worlds tunnel, shift, dance, and get haircuts. When your mind slips off, it forgets to distinguish between them, so they leak through and stain each other.

A buzz.

I'm on Erica's couch and we're both naked. I massage her wings, leftover from the beach. "I have the perfect words," she whispers in my ear.

What are they?

"Saddle, cupcake, jellyfish."

I know she's right because as soon as they begin to form in my mouth they melt away into a fog of mystery. It has a sweet aftertaste, I tell her.

"So you haven't asked how we got here," she comments, a sly grin sliding across her face.

A buzz happened.

"The sounds space makes when the things floating in it pop in and out of existence in one place or another."

72?

"That is all."

72 cracks in the sidewalk

          between Emerson Avenue

             and Main Street.

   I watch helplessly as the front

tire of my bicycle rolls

lazily over all of them.

   Weather meets concrete and

            war happens.

   Concrete looses and cracks.

   Life falls in between the cracks

     and grows into

         shy little shrubberies.

Concrete asserts itself,

suffocating them,

     but sooner or later,

       weather wins again.

Arnold the alien with ideas for arms asks me to tell him a story.

"It's been years since I've heard a good story," he says without moving his lips. When he says a year, I don't really know what length of time he's talking about. He probably doesn't either. I think he's heard me say *year* before. Arnold's arms sway back and forth as wispy willow trees. I ask if he's ever seen a willow tree and he asks me what a willow tree is.

You're imagining it perfectly.

I decide to tell Arnold a true story about a witch. She's very tin and pale and floats slowly with her arms outstretched to her sides. She says nothing but emanates terror.

"She sounds beautiful," says Arnold thoughtfully.

I tell Arnold she is, but that's not the

point. I tell him back when she was a young girl, she fell into a black pool of sorrow and insecurity. No one put it there on purpose and no one tried to lure her into it. All of the fairies in the forest she lived in with her family would cry from time to time. When fairies cry, their emotions leak out with their tears. When they cry tears of joy, their tears drift up in shades of green and yellow and orange and sometimes even red and purple and become leaves on old trees. When they cry tears of sorrow and insecurity, their tears trickle down in the little black streams that found their way to this pool the witch fell into.

When she came up, the pool was gone. All the black, liquid fairy sorrow absorbed into her, now her burden to carry. Now, having absorbed all of this sorrow and insecurity, the witch got symptoms. She got the blues, then she got angry, then she got paranoid, and finally be became vengeful. You see, I tell Arnold, with that much sorrow and insecurity, her mind became sick and suddenly she began blaming her accident on others and believed they were all deserving of cruel punishment.   Now she clings to these feelings as her source of dark power.

I want to get through to her, show her that forgiveness will help her more than hunting Aima and me ever will. Arnold asks who Aima is.

The spaceship drops me off on Aima's lawn just as her mother is running out the door to make an appointment she told me about last week.

"What the fuck!"

I'm in a heap on the lawn as the spaceship streaks away.

I tell her I fell.

"Bullshit!"

I…I really can't explain this one.

She nods nervously and says she'll be back in two hours.

Aima must have seen everything from the window. She runs out of the house and plops herself down next to me.

"Whoosh!" she exclaims, flinging her little arms outward and back in again. "Whoa, what just happened? I can't remember anything!" She speaks as if from a script in tiny print.

I don't know, the last thing I saw was a bright flash of light, and then here we are.

"We have to stop the witch," Aima decides.

For once and for all?

"Yes."

How are we going to do that?

"Don't worry, I have a plan."

72 gallons in a large bathtub.

72 birds flying south. I saw them one cold October morning lifting up from a cornfield in Illinois, swarming and squawking until suddenly order came of their chaos and they flew away in a nice, tidy V.

72 stitches make up the circumference of the hat Erica is knitting for her niece.

It's baby colors—pastel blues, greens, yellows and a hint of orange—even though the kid's eight.

She's trying to learn to knit the way you wrap the slack yarn around your index finger and hold it above the project, gathering a loop from above for every stitch. A woman on a plane told her she'd be able to knit much quicker and with tighter stitches if she mastered this. Erica tries every once in a while, but shortly gives up.

"I made patient soup yesterday," she tells me, rebelliously dropping her index finger and knitting her way. We are on my moon boat on Neptune. I'm quite popular over here. It's been difficult to find some time to spend with just Erica. Even as we left the dock to set sail over the blue and green gas ocean, three other boaters tried to seduce me over for cocktails. You drink cocktails on Neptune from snow globes and spit out the Santas.

How long did it take?

"Ten minutes. I made it thinking about patience and putting patient energy into it."

You don't have any patient energy to begin with.

"I ate it right back up after."

So you're just as patient as you were before.

Erica puts down her knitting to take off her life jacket.

I ask her what her niece's name is.

"Persephone."

The divine daughter who gets lured down into the underworld and eats three pomegranate seeds. Now part of the underworld is in her and she has to come back at least to visit. It seems like less a binding curse and more of an inclination. Once you've ingested a place, you wonder how it's holding up while you're gone.

Erica and I drift over waves of thick, Neptunian gas, shifting and churning under little streaks of moonlight. Neptunian sea creatures play beneath the surface. An octopredian leaps out from the depths, flips majestically through the air and dives back in. Octopredians have eight tentacles, like any proper earth octopus. Except their faces look like dolphins, they have an eye at the end of each tentacle and they sing love ballads.

"That's romantic," Erica giggles.

It's good luck.

I like to say things are good luck to see if I'll actually believe it. When I do, good things tend to happen. When I don't, I tend to forget about it and don't notice anything special. Erica taught me this. You get what you believe is coming if you're expectations aren't too specific.

Aima brings me to the witch's house. It's an old oak tree in the meadow between the edge of her backyard and the playground. There's a hole in the trunk where you'd picture an owl perching or a squirrel nesting. Its skin is thick and dark and cracked in dramatic lines, twisting and crunching around a thick trunk and branches. All the leaves are gone, leaving a naked, death-like figure standing alone in the meadow. The sun sets slowly behind it, slouching down to touch a grassy horizon.

"This is where the witch lives," says Aima.

Do you think she's home?

My heart thumps a quick baseline for the rave in my chest cavity. Arteries stomp.

"No, we have to set a trap."

Aima wants to surround the tree with a thick layer of blackberry brambles and put a spell on them that would make the witch think they were broomsticks. She will try to ride on them and get hurt.

That will just make her angrier.

"And then when she's too hurt to walk, we catch her in a net and kill her."

But if we kill the witch without killing her grudge first, it will have to go somewhere. Grudges like that are so powerful they don't just go away when their vessel dies.

Aima looks puzzled.

If a ship sinks, the people in it can sail away on lifeboats and go be people somewhere else. If the witch dies, the grudge can just go be a grudge somewhere else, and since we'll be the closest ones to it—not to mention we'll be extra susceptible because we'd have just done something that people carrying grudges do—it will just go into us and we'll be miserable and evil.

"What's a grudge?"

Something you stay mad about until it makes you really sick and sometimes it gets contagious.

Aima thinks for a minute, pursing her lips and glancing up at the tree.

"If we don't kill her, what can we do?"

We have to dissolve the grudge.

The same way someone dissolved all my stuff.

The same way someone dissolved my apartment, my cat, my fridge, my toilet, my big solid things.

The same way someone dissolved my grudge.

72 fairies in the woods the witch used to play in as a child before she fell into the black pool of despair.

72 fairies with

72 sets of wings and

72 pairs of eyes that leak sometimes when their little bodies are overwhelmed with sorrow and insecurity.

72 fairies at the ball.

72 stitches make up the circumference of Persephone's hat—the hat she wears down to Hell and up to Heaven.

The hat she wears when she

wonders how the other is doing.

The hat stained with drops of pomegranate juice.

She lets the lord of the

underworld borrow it sometimes when

his head gets cold.

72. That is all.

Erica and I had to abandon ship. My moon boat scraped the back of an iguanopod. Iguanopods have sharp razors on the shells they wear on their backs to ward off predators. Their faces kind of look like iguanas and they are adamant pacifists. To this day, iguanopods have unanimously opposed every Neptunian war, even though no one has ever asked their opinion. Now we're in a tiny lifeboat drifting across the Neptunian ocean.

"Someone's bound to come and rescue us, seeing as how you're very popular," she teases.

I shrug.

"How do you think it happened?" she asks, shifting around to rub my back of wispy blankets on a cold winter night.

How what happened?

"How all your stuff vanished and you

stopped speaking with your lips."

I didn't realize this.

"It's nothing to be ashamed of. I rather like it."

I think it dissolved.

"There's nothing you see right now or ever that's not already completely dissolved into the space surrounding it," says Erica. "Before, you were just looking in other places."

The one man in an entire stadium blinking in and out of existence instead of wide-open spaces.

"Exactly."

She rolls lazily over the side of our little boat and disappears beneath the gaseous waves.

Erica doesn't need anyone to rescue her. Rumor has it, she fell straight through the planet's core and out the other side, through the window of a spaceship and now she's barreling through space in search of the Milky Way's long lost twin sister, Powder Path. She's a pathway of sparkly space dust and loves trashy romance novels. Everyone living in her galaxy is cosmically dramatic and horny. Erica's aliens are brilliant, brown bear-sized space slugs. They're large and slimy and play classical music with their minds, which they keep in one giant, communal jar which fuels their spaceship.

"But yet you feel the need to rescue the witch?"

I'm not alone on my tiny boat anymore. From the depths, a spiralfish (pretty self-explanatory except when they leave the ocean, they assume the shape of the greatest fear of whoever they come in contact with first) leapt up and transformed into a thin, extremely pale and terrifyingly made-up woman with jet black eyes and arms outstretched to her sides.

Now she's right beside me in the life boat. I feel her grudge rub up against me and it itches.

"It wouldn't hurt so bad if there was nothing for the grudge to rub up against," she suggests through pungent red lips.

My arms curl into a walrus with a toothache.

I trust Erica to not need rescuing; the witch is sick and crippled and cannot help herself and will hurt and infect others unless she is stopped.

I sound like Aima.

"And how do you propose to stop her?"

I tell the spiralfish I need to dissolve her grudge.

"How will you dissolve something you did not create and cannot touch without bleeding?"

Itching.

"Whatever."

The spiralfish shifts into a six-year-old girl named Aima.

"Ah, now I see."

What's there to see? I'm terrified of a six-year-old sociopath that's made up of tiny little specks existing from time to time in wide-open spaces simply because those specks still have something worth living for. I'm terrified of playing her game and I'm terrified that she imagined it.

The spiralfish giggles and splashes me with a powdery trickle of gaseous ocean. I dip my hand in to sprinkle her back, but something grabs my wrist and pulls me in.

I land in Aima's tree house in her backyard. Her dad built it for her. The tree house is decorated in pastel streamers and some toys scattered here and there. Aima lets go of my wrist and demands, "What's a sociopath?"

Someone who tells lies for fun.

"Like Dr. Seuss?"

No, not like Dr. Seuss.

"So those stories are true?" she asks, eyes wide with delight and wonder.

Yes. Completely.

72 stories

and none of

them are true.

Some

of

them

should

be.

72 instances

for a plot to

develop out of

thin air.

Erica used to write stories about murders. I remember one scene where the killer gets cornered by the Nancy Drew-like heroine on the dock of a lake, and lakes are huge when you're seven. The heroine demands, "Stop!" but of course the killer knows he—or she, Erica never specified—will go to jail, which is probably more boring than death, so the killer puts the gun in his or her mouth and shoots the back of his or her head off. The teacher knew Erica wrote it, but we were all too young to realize what it looked like for an adult to be concerned.

72 songs that pluck my heartstrings like the veins of a sun god. Clink clank clunk. Suddenly a song traces its fingertips across the sunset. I'm sitting on top of a mountain with Arnold the alien with ideas for arms. Space is purple up here, and stars twinkle shy shades of silver from far away

and probably millions of years ago.

Arnold asks me what a good beer tastes like. I tell him it tastes like the most refreshing slice of toast in the galaxy. He doesn't believe me.

"I was a blanket for a while," Arnold says. "I was all yarn and loops. I could feel all parts of my being intertwined from a single train of thought. Someone kept coming back to the same thought over and over again and suddenly I was a blanket."

What happened?

"I snagged on a nail and unraveled. Then all of my things became unreal."

I was a lamp and my bulb burned out, then all my things became unreal.

I was a tree on the side of a mountain that became a volcano and erupted, then all my things became unreal.

I was a roof on a 300-year-old house that caved in one day, then all my things became unreal.

I was a meadow and a farmer plowed me and planted soybeans, then all my things became unreal.

I was a sweater that snagged on a nail in the doorway and unraveled, then all my things became unreal. I was the blanket's favorite cousin. We watched trashy vampire shows and told secrets.

We pass a black hole in space, somewhere between here and there.

"She's heartbroken," says Arnold.

Who is?

"An old star. That's what happens when a star is heartbroken."

A gaping hole in space forms and sucks everything it touches into its black depths to never come out again. I ask who broke her heart and Arnold confesses it was he. Arnold's arms swirl into black wisps of remorse.

I wonder what it's like to have history with a star.

"Dramatic."

Aima says the witch is a sociopath. I have to watch what I say around that girl. No, I tell her. The witch has never lied to us. She's mean, but she's real fucking honest about it.

I have to stop swearing in front of Aima, too.

"She lies about everything."

Like what?

"She made the flowers have teeth and bite us, but they look like flowers that don't bite us so she lied."

That's not a lie, that's a strategy.

Aima shrugs. We are in her room rummaging through her toy chest in search of tools to dissolve the witch's grudge. So far, Aima has pulled out an Aladdin doll, which can rub the grudge and turn it into a genie and then we can wish for it to dissolve. She also has a magnifying glass, but instead of making things bigger, this special glass makes things smaller so we can shrink the grudge before we turn it into a genie. There will be less grudge to dissolve and less chance it can overpower us if it decides to be a bad genie. Either way, it will have to grant our wish. That's what genies do.

Aima wants to lure the witch into a hole in the ground before we go for her grudge, but she says that will be hard because the witch can fly, so we'll have to put a spell on her broom so it only flies down.

"We'll cover the hole with a spell that makes it look like the ground so the witch walks right over it and falls in," Aima says. "You have to distract her and lead her into the hole."

She's looks like my nightmare, you know.

"That's why you're the only one she'll go after."

Aima got into a fight with a fairy while we played witch. It was when we were turned evil but didn't know it so we thought evil was good. She tried to pull off a fairy's wings, cackling and taunting the fairy.

"You're so tiny and stupid, there's nothing you can do about it!"

But I have magical powers to turn your fingers oily so you won't be able to grasp anything you try to hold! I declared in my tiniest, most fairy-like voice.

Aima turned to me, crossed her arms across her chest and pouted.

We're good again, I told her solemnly. If you try to kill a fairy, she'll turn you good because she knows that's the only way to stop an evil act.

"That's not how it works!" she pouted.

Then how does it work? I asked her.

Aima pouted some more.

A buzz.

Wade becomes a blanket. I am cold and he finds me sitting on the stoop of our old house. The sidewalk beneath the last step splits open and shy little shrubberies peek out. My feet like the idea. They become wispy green leaves hovering just above the pavement. The shrubs know something's not quite right.

Being approached by a blanket caught in a peculiar updraft is rather awkward.

Wade floats down the street, waits at the stoplight for passing cars to halt, then proceeds down the sidewalk, past the church next door. He floats up the front walk and wraps himself snug around me. I smell him like late at night. Stale beer and tobacco, daytime still clinging to him. Seaweed scented hair.

Still keeping that buzz going?

"Kid, I'll be nursing this beer till the day I die," he chuckles, fringes jiggling.

How did you find me here?

"That trippy arm of yours snagged on a jagged edge of an asteroid on your way down from the stars, it's been unraveling ever since. I just followed the trail right to you."

Like Hansel and Gretel.

"Like a puppy to a fire hydrant."

Like a pair of spectacles to the sun.

We watch as the sun reaches out with solar flared arms and catches a giant pair of sunglasses mid-eclipse.   Dusk falls over Australia in the morning.

Wade unravels, turns copper, and weaves himself into an overflowing teacup. I slurp gently off the top. I tell him he's my giving tree and he chuckles ripples.

"Kid, you'll never catch me giving up all my leaves and branches."

Wade says he's good at the afterlife because he got a head start. He'd been the living dead for years.   Spirits even recognized him when he finally croaked. The deadest man alive, they called him. A man who could single-handedly peel back one dimension and lay it on top of another long enough to crawl through and scurry back. Just this one time, it snapped shut, slicing him in two.

"When that happens, you gotta choose one side or the other, and the only side in which all of you can survive is death," says Wade. "If you cling to life in death, you'll be cosmically itchy. Even the most comfortable couch will feel a bit off, and no matter how many times you reposition yourself, you'll never feel quite right. Everything you say will sound awkward to your own ears and you'll regret every decision you make even if you were right."

Wade wanted the freedom to know he was right, to be stubborn, to float from one form to the next, to plop into the universe's most comfortable couch and feel absolutely whole.

72 teddy bears in a

daycare center.

72 tiny sets of arms

and legs to hug and

scratch and run.

72 colors in a

rainbow

drifting through

the Milky Way.

72 dragonflies buzzing over

the crystal surface of a very

large puddle.

To some, it accumulated from this morning's

rain and will be gone in a few hours when

the sun comes out. To others, it's antiquity.

72. *That is all.*

A buzz.

I am sitting in front of Aima's costume chest. Her entire face and torso are immersed in dresses, wigs and tool belts, little legs kicking up over the side. I am decorated in a far-too-small Snow White dress, a pink bob wig, and Mardi Gras beads. She's dressing me up as bait.

"The Snow White dress will remind her of her witch-friend's stepdaughter so she'll come and try to finish you off. The pink bob wig makes her come faster so she won't have time to see where she's going, and the Mardi Gras beads have the power to transform you into an inch worm to confuse her just in case anything goes wrong in our perfect plan," Aima explains.

I am terrified.

Aima stretches all the way down to the bottom of her chest and resurfaces with an absurdly gold, shiny cloak. She studies it intently, shrugs, then throws it back in the trunk. She says an invisibility cloak would be counterproductive. I taught her that word a month ago when she was ready to take a nap but wanted to eat a Pixie Stick.

"You have to tell her she doesn't scare you so she tries to scare you more," Aima says. "She gets more powerful when other people are afraid of her so when you tell her you're not afraid you have to act like you really, really mean it so she takes you seriously and tries to hurt you to prove she's really scary.

"Like this, 'You mean old witch, you don't scare me at all! You're funny, ugly, and I kind of like you!'

Yeah, tell her you like her and try to mean it."

A buzz.

Arnold the alien with ideas for arms pats me on the back with long sweater sleeves. He knows I'm drunk and he knows I can't remember why. He says he picked me up at the edge of the solar system on a moon so stubborn it didn't even need a planet to orbit.

I'm not exactly sure what I want to be yet and I know I will be in time if I just stop fixating on what I will never ever be able to have right now.

Erica speaks through me like a cowgirl with two broken legs. Her tears run down my cheeks from galaxies away.

Arnold's arms turn guilty and I tell him he has nothing to feel guilty about. He blushes in shades of blue. I am in a constant state of blushing these days.

He says, "There's no reason to ever feel guilty about what is because here we are. If it were some other way, that's where we'd be, so cheer up."

He knows I'm not convinced, and I don't think he is either.

"It's just that sometimes what is sucks anyways," he sighs.

It's not all good, but all will change.

"Simple to say, hard to believe."

Simple to believe, hard to feel when things suck, which is when you've got to feel it most.

Arnold shrugs, shaking off ripples of bright red thought yarns. One disconnects and weaves itself into a skyscraper far away and long ago from us.

"But it is all my fault," Arnold admits.

What is?

"Why all your stuff became unreal and now you're on a cosmic roller coaster."

I like it though.

Arnold smiles in that defeated kind of way. "You don't remember the first time you were sucked through a black hole, but I do."

What do you mean?

"I tried to bring you through again so many times to make it right, but I know I can't undo what's been done."

Is that why I've been bouncing around so much?

I already know the answer. So what happened in the first place?

"First," Arnold chuckles. "No, not first, but everywhen and sometime I became a cigarette. You were smoking me. You remember, don't you?"

At the haunted house with Erica years ago.

"Yes," he says. "And when I told you I broke that star's heart, and when a star's heart breaks it becomes a black hole that sucks everything and everyone who touches it into the opposite of existence?"

Yes.

"So, you know how you and I and Erica and everything become things across the universe in places familiar and alien?"

Yes.

Arnold begs me to stop agreeing with him and I agree. He is flustered. His arms spiral into chaos.

"Stars are the same, and she was the house. I burned between your fingers and lips and her heart broke because it reminded her of how she'd burned down and the family that perished inside."

But all my stuff didn't become unreal until recently. It wasn't spontaneous on the spot. That happened years ago. I don't know what years ago means anymore.

"Spontaneous things sometimes take quite a while to unfold."

It's not your fault, Arnold. You just happened to be there and she just happened to be affected, like a watermelon plant just happening to shoot off a vine to support itself on a carrot that just can't take the weight.

"Just like a watermelon."

72 watermelon vines in the poly-tunnel on a small farm in South Wales. Tom the farm manager tells me to gently but boldly untangle them after peeling and washing the onions. "The onion," Tom says, "is tangible meditation. Peel away all the outer layers and when you get to the center of your being, you find your true essence. Nothing."

But the peel is juicy like

grapefruit and gossip.

72 houses in the neighborhood. One of them just happened to burn down.

72 cigarettes lit in that same neighborhood. One of them just happened to be mine. One of them just happened to be Arnold. He says for the most part humans can only see human cross-sections of our more cosmic selves. Beings like Arnold are different. They can see more of what they always are all at once.

72, that is all.

In Arnold's handwriting.

I am a worm wriggling on a hook. Aima is the fisherman. She holds the magic *p* that can also be a *q*, *b*, or *d* to confuse the witch just in case. I am fucking terrified.

Aima leads me out to the hammock in the back of the park, just beyond the point where neatly trimmed grass meets thick forest, down a foot-trodden path and into a clearing between a few very large pine trees. It's not as cold back here because the forest creates a wall blocking the wind. It smells of decadence and mildew. Green, yellow, orange, and sometimes red and purple leaves crisp and rot. I lay in the hammock and Aima scurries up a nearby tree.

I shift uncomfortably, glancing around the forest unable to see past the first jagged ring of trees and underbrush. She could be anywhere and she's always everywhere. Aima is impatient. I look up at her apologetically.

"Say something!"

I shift around so my feet push the hammock outward as far as it can go around the middle and sway in almost-unbalanced limbo. I scream out in a broken voice, "I'm not afraid of you and you are ugly." My lips move, chords twitch, warm vibrating air rising from my stomach, into my throat and out my lips. My heart skips a beat. I hold my hands out in front of me. Solid. I clear my throat.

"You're not really all that evil, and I'm not afraid of you!"

Aima is silent.

"In fact, I like you a lot!"

Aima is silent.

"I am NOT afraid of you!"

Aima is silent. No, Aima is gone.

I jump out of the hammock, pink bob

askew. Slowing her down might be a good thing at this point. "Aima!"

No answer.

"Aima?"

A scatter of ambiguous p's, q's, d's and b's around the base of the trunk of her tree. A ripped invisibility cloak. A clue.

72, that is all.

Through the trees and out into the park. Playground, swing set, picnic tables, wide-open field, no Aima. Looking for the one familiar little girl in a wide-open space and she is nowhere to be found. Erica perches on a swing.

"I found Powder Path," says Erica, kicking up a mound of sand with her foot.

"How was it?"

"Dramatic."

She smells like space slime and her wings are still glazed in it.

"Good conversations though," she shrugs. "I got the blues."

"I hear even cowgirls get them."

She smiles down at her lap, then glances up at me. "I've been barreling through the universe in search of a place to make my home, but it's been here the whole time. Patient soup my ass. How've you been?"

"Arnold stopped bringing me through wormholes and my arms are flesh and my voice works again."

"Apparently."

"And the witch took Aima," I explain, holding up the clue. A large piece of birch bark with a scribbled message. Not in Arnold's handwriting. I have a pocket full of p's and q's and b's and d's. Or maybe just a pocket full of p's and q's to be minded, depending on how they've shifted against the fabric.

"I guess this is when we finally get to play Witch," says Erica.

"I guess so."

Erica asks how we play and I say we can do anything as long as we explain it. The first course of action is to either find where the witch took Aima, or to lure her to where we are. Seeing as she's kidnapped Aima, she obviously knew of our plan and foiled it, and she wants to lure me to where she is.

"Then she would have left an obvious clue as to where she is, or at least as to where the trap is," Erica reasons.

72 houses in the neighborhood,

just one of them happened to burn down.

72 cigarettes smoking in the neighborhood,

one of them just happened to be
Arnold in my mouth.

72 fairies in the woods crying
tears of despair
into a pool the witch fell into.

72 broken hearts in the galaxy
(on a very, very, very good day).

One witch,
one house,
one star.

One wormhole.

"We have to go to the haunted house."

"The one by my parents' house that burned down?" asks Erica.

She asks if we can hitch a ride from Arnold and I say I don't know how to get a hold of him.

"Well we can make it up if we just explain it, right?"

Only if he's playing, too.

"Let's just hope it's a very, very, very good day in the galaxy."

I take the *p*'s and *q*'s and *b*'s and *d*'s out of my pocket and hand them to Erica. She arranges them in a circle in the sand, round parts to the center with the straight ends jutting out to the right. She draws a small circle between the round heads in the sand with her finger and pulls down her pants.

"When I **pee** in the middle, they all

become **p**'s, but they're really strong **p**'s because everyone knows **p**'s are very easily persuaded," explains Erica. "When I **p**ee in the circle, you have to **p**olitely request the **p**'s to become a **p**ortal large enough to fit us. You have to ask it to be a **p**ortal because they can't logically become anything that doesn't begin with the letter **p**. It's not in their nature."

She's good.

Erica thinks of something wet and dripping, like a faucet or a waterfall, and lets it go. "**P**retty, **p**ink and **p**urple **p**lush **p**lease be a **p**ortal to Arnold's spaceship," I coo, in my sweetest, most sugary voice.

Erica finishes.

The *p*'s glow bright orange and let out a pink ray of light. Erica grabs my hand and pulls me into the beam.

A buzz.

Arnold sits next to me on a bright yellow couch woven of pulsing idea threads. Erica is making coffee. Arnold found a coffee pot in the Artic Circle last year around Christmas. I wonder whose wish it was. Coffee doesn't like to be in space and protests violently, leaping out of their mugs in long lava lamp clumps. Arnold's arms swirl into figs growing off an icicle.

"So you want me to give you a ride to

the haunted house?" he asks.

Yes.

I am so done with quotation marks.

"And there you will…"

Turn the witch's grudge into a genie and with it to dissolve itself.

"I see."

But first we have to lure the witch into a hole and shrink the grudge so it becomes a small genie.

"You know, that plan didn't quite work the first time."

Yeah, about that…

"She's imagining too."

A buzz.

Wade is being a tree house, staggering slightly in the wind. His tree is 72 years old. 72 rings to prove it, but you can't see them unless you cut it down. 72, that is all.

"Aima's onto something, you know," says Wade in woody creaks.

Of course she is.

"With the whole kill-her-with-kindness thing. She's fucking powerful, but only if you hand over your head and your mind with it."

A stubborn moon without a planet.

In a tree so stubborn it grows from a plastic green turtle-shaped sand box just because the lilac bush said it couldn't be done.

Is that how I'm supposed to dissolve her grudge?

"Simplest way's usually right."

And the hardest.

"The hard part's getting past yourself."

That awful little voice wondering very loudly what the fuck is so wrong with me that I can't even do the simplest thing right.

"That stupid little voice of yours doesn't know a carrot from an elephant and thinks simple and easy are one in the same."

Like dragons and zebras.

"Like nails and fossils."

A bird perches on the branch outside the tree house window. She's yellow with an orange top hat and only shits on convertibles and children eating ice cream cones.

"What you've got to remember," says Wade, "is not to be so hard on yourself. So let whatever it is you're feeling just be, and know you're doing great."

A buzz.

Erica beams down behind a truck stop gas station on the way to the haunted house. Arnold wants to try the most refreshing slice of toast in the galaxy before facing his ex.

"I burned between your lips for a few minutes, but in that time we were tall grass on a prairie and two twigs off the same branch. She was the most beautiful star in my Milky Way, and I was the sexiest ring around her planet. We loved passionately for those few minutes and forever until she discovered, somewhere deep within our love, a memory of a fire that destroyed her."

And you can't break someone's heart without breaking a bit of yours too. The jagged shards of one heart fly off from impact and cut the other.

"Bitterness is like pointing a salty finger into a wound. I hear booze helps."

Wade once said there are just some things you're better off being numb to.

"Think he mistook numbness for detachment."

Where do you draw the line between Buddhist and junkie?

"You've got to really hate something to need to numb yourself to everything around you just to avoid it, and really attached to something to have to numb your pain when it leaves."

Too many needles dropped into the most comfortable couch in the world to sit on without an iron suit.

"Pull the needles out or get a new couch."

Arnold sips one of those seasonal autumn beers with an orangey label and some pumpkins. Erica's munching a bag of chips and I've lost my appetite.

"Now that's a refreshing slice of toast if I ever drank one."

Arnold slipped through one evening into a perpendicular dimension where people drink solids and scoop gases. Their eyes, ears, and skin grow inside their bodies so all they can see, hear and touch is within. They love it when flowers bloom indoors during the winter.

We fly low over Erica's parents' house and swoop into a parking lot a few blocks over from the haunted house. It's a proper haunted day outside. The wind is blowing like it knows us and leaves tumble at our heels. We exit off an extendable ramp and trudge down the middle of the street. I have no costumes, no props, and no weapons. Erica's fingers a grease stained and Arnold is a bit tipsy.

The haunted house is all charred shingles and peeling paint. All the windows are boarded up and it's surrounded by a chain-link fence with a big **NO TRESPASSING** sign nailed ominously to a tree by the front gate. Her branches reach out into the sky like jack-o-lantern arms to the east. Her west is burnt off. She balances her gimp with terror. Erica shivers.

"I feel her," she murmurs.

The witch watches us climb the fence

with charred shutter lashes.

Her front door opens and shuts in the wind revealing Aima tied to a rickety rocking chair in the entrance hallway. Her eyes scream but her words are frozen.

"You know she put you out front as bait because she's just as scared as you are. She had her guard down and believed in me more in that moment than ever before," explains the witch.

Shutters halt and a violent breeze tears through the house and out the front door. Black wisps wind into a tall, pale woman with arms outstretched and jet black eyes. Her hair is pulled back into a frigid bun and her lips glow sunset red. She kisses Arnold on the cheek and twirls his enamored arm around a long, pointy finger.

72 houses in the neighborhood,

           one just happened to burn down.

72 little girls

playing in the woods,

one just happened to

fall into the black pool of despair.

           72 leaves on a very small tree.

      72 potential splinters on a branch.

72 prehistoric puddles.

                72, that is all.

"That is everything," says the witch.

I guess it really just depends on what you mean by the same word.

"All."

I shrug.

"So how are you going to dissolve my grudge?" she asks. "Only I can dissolve my grudge and that I just will not do."

Gives you power and purpose but makes you miserable.

"Most people are miserable anyways without the benefits of power and purpose," she says. "I'll take my chances with misery."

Arnold lifts his eyes to meet hers but she is not paying attention. Erica runs over and rubs his shoulders. "Don't let her break your heart," she whispers.

The witch dissolves and reappears behind Erica, except now she looks like a very large snail. "I'll dissolve my grudge just like you'll dissolve your guilt."

Erica was three and barely beginning to understand who was alive and who was not. Snails were not. They slid in slime and made lovely crunching noises when broken underfoot. Her parents had a snail problem in their garden and encouraged her. Years later, she realized what she'd actually done. In that moment, the lives of others became worlds.

72 snails out for a walk. Tiny Erica steps on five of them. One just happened to be the witch…the rest were her sisters.

So this is what happens when you fall into a black pool of despair.

"You experience what it feels like to cry like a fairy over and over and over."

It's easy to say *that is all* when it's not slowly peeling away at your skin.

A buzz.

I am in the parking lot at the mall in my hometown, about a mile from Erica's parents' house. I'm sitting at the only picnic bench in the parking lot, which wouldn't make sense unless I was dreaming. Parked cars linger, but they're all asleep and covered in snow, but it is midsummer and flowers with teeth sprout up from cracks in the pavement below our feet. One of them was once an A sharp. Another sings only in C notes. Aima and I sit on top of the table as flowers snap at our feet. Blood squirts from just below her elbow. She has been bit.

"The witch turned us evil because these flowers are infected with evil and evil is contagious. And then I bit you and now we're on the witch's side and she wants us to kill all the fairies in the forest," explains Aima.

We're not going to kill any fairies, Aima.

There's a deep gash on my leg with Aima-sized teeth marks.

"But we have to, we don't know the difference."

And here comes the witch.

She's floating towards us, arms outstretched as always. We are trapped on the table and Aima thinks we're evil. The witch traps me with jet black eyes and I gaze back. Nothing. Nothing. Nothing. I try to remember the rules of the game, anything is possible as long as I explain it…nothing.

"You ought to listen to her," says the witch. "She knows how to play the game."

There's no such thing as absolute good and evil.

"But yet she moves fluidly between them."

You can't move through brick walls just like that.

"But Aima can."

She is more than any phase of matter, she seeps through tiny cracks where even renegade shrubs cannot.

"Light as a feather but taller than trees."

The witch is upon us. She touches my face with icy hands and brings her sunset red lips to mine.

A buzz.

72 fairies dance naked around the fire. They have no idea we are hiding behind a jagged grass tree. The witch has us in pointy hats and striped stockings. I know she plans to frame us for murdering the fairies, but I am evil and so is Aima. My heart is full and I know my actions will go unpunished. A warm tingle fills me from head to toe, but then I realize this feeling is fleeting. Am I really happy? Then fear. I see happy

dancing fairies and wonder why I'm not a happy dancing fairy. Would I be happier were I a happy dancing fairy? I want to steal their happiness for myself and put it in a sack to munch on later when my happiness fades.

"I want you to cast a spell over the fire to leap out and burn all the fairies alive," says the witch. She and Aima are imagining.

"But that will burn up all the fear, which makes us stronger," explains Aima. "And it burns up all the happiness so we can't put it in our sack to munch on later."

The witch thinks for a moment.

"Then we will confound them by shooting confusion at them from the tips of our hats and hack off their wings with our enchanted daggers."

Aima likes this idea but worries she is not strong enough. The witch casts a spell on her to make her as strong as three horses. I muster up all the confusion I can imagine in the tip of my hat but at the last moment I wonder if I've done it right. Is it confusion or disorientation? Is it neither? Can I do anything right? Can I even imagine without second-guessing myself? I wonder how the witch manages to imagine with so much evil floating inside of her.

Aima shoots the fairies with confusion pouring out the tip of her hat and they freeze in terror, unable to imagine what to do. The witch rushes forward, enchanted dagger in hand, spewing nightmares and broken promises. Erica's wings are beautiful but I can't speak them. The witch has wings. They are ominous but glowing. She lunges at a fairy. Aima's wings are shades of blue and orange, shy but smiling. She has the perfect words…

"But if you try to kill a fairy, it turns you good because she knows that's the only way to really stop and evil act," says Aima, glancing back at me and winking. "It's just the way fairies are, even when they're confused."

A buzz.

I wake up on Erica's couch. She is making tea in the kitchen and I'm wondering if my apartment has returned. The smooth scent of rose creeps around the corner and into the living room, preceding sleep-eyed Erica in panties and a shawl. Was it all just a dream? I hate when stories end like that.

"Arnold's still asleep," says Erica, lifting my legs, sitting, and bringing them down over her. "He was exhausted when we got back, so I'm just going to let the dude sleep."

I ask what happened.

"You and Aima and the witch disappeared and Arnold and I just sat there for a long time at the haunted house," she says. "We felt low, like nothing would ever be alright ever again, it was terrible."

But then the funk lifted and they realized everything was fine.

Erica pushes the blanket aside and snuggles up under my arm. Her hair smells of ginger and her fingers dance under my shirt across my stomach. "It wasn't quite meant to be, but it happened somehow, and here we are," she whispers. "Isn't that nice?"

I walk the six blocks back to my apartment. Fridge buzzing, cat meowing for food, and toilet flushing just fine. My dresser, shoved full of clothes, bed unmade, and dirty dishes fill my sink. I wash them, brush my teeth, and leave to play with Aima. Now I'm sitting on her front lawn and she's in my lap, painting fresh butterflies on my cheeks. She does not want to play Witch today.

"How can we play Witch?" she asks matter-of-factly.

So she really is gone.

"We tricked her into dissolving her own grudge, but first I tricked you into believing you were evil," she giggles, her little eyes glowing with mischief.

Why did you do that?

Aima smiles and says nothing.

I ask whatever happened to the witch.

"She decided to go off with those slug aliens to live in Powder Path," says Aima. "She took a very friendly spaceship."

I ask if it was too stubborn to run on fuel.

"Arnold gave it the most refreshing slice of toast in the galaxy."

The Beginning

About the Author

Rebecca believes the most unbelievable, utterly fantastic stories are all true, even if they never really happened. Inspiration sneaks up on her in unlikely places and sometimes and spontaneous events sometimes take quite a while to unfold. Rebecca loves aliens, ghosts, cryptos, and all other lurkers and firmly believes that when in doubt, make your own damn genre. For her next trick, she aspires to write a saucy series of bedtime stories for grown-ups.

When Water Meets Herself

A Bonus Short Story from

Rebecca Little

(Because she thinks you're kind of cool.)

He asked me if I'd like to see how a storm is planted. I said sure.

I met Earl on karaoke night. I was living out in Utah on a seasonal gig, counting spotted owls for the Forest Service. I'm in the business of counting things. I started out counting plants, pulling seasonal gigs as a botanist but with the help of some fudged credentials, security clearance, and field experience, I made the shift over to wildlife surveys. Now I'm in owls. Now I'm in central Utah where everyone's got a theory and a plan B, and every night is karaoke night.

He sat in the seat next to me at the bar. I had just polished off my third whiskey sour in hopes of mustering the courage to sing but instead I spent the night talking to Earl. He asked me what I had against my own voice that I wouldn't get up and go sing and I said I'd rather use it to talk to him. So we talked and he asked me if I'd like to see how a storm is planted. I told him I didn't get many days off since I worked a seasonal job, so why should I spend one of them watching storms get planted and he told me the reason.

"Water don't lie," said Earl. "Doesn't know how, it's not in its nature. Buddha knew it and now you do too. You want to know the truth, go look at some water."

So I agreed. The night before my next day off, I called Earl on the number he'd written on the receipt for the beer I'd bought for him and he said he'd come pick me up in the morning which he did. We drove his rig south along the western edge of the San Rafael Swell, an expanse of high desert uplift with landforms fit for some other planet.

He asked me why I trusted him enough to get in his pick-up. Me, a young lady with a degree and some nice legs if he did say so himself. Him, scraggly and stuck in Central Utah. I told him his eyes were blue like the water that didn't know how to lie. I told him I was packing a knife just in case. My eyes have never been blue.

We drove along a highway carved through time, layers of rock formations rising up in sheets of millions of years. I asked him if he was talking about cloud seeding. My neighbor said they seeded clouds in the San Rafael Swell to research its uses in weather warfare, climate control and ski resorts. My neighbor said shit's going to hit the fan in a big way because of it. Her eyes got really big and serious behind her thick glasses and she told me you can't tell Mother Nature what to do. You can't make her snow when she wanted to save her water for later. You can't make a cloud bleed with silver iodide or dry ice or some shit just because your fucking ski resort needs some powder on it. She told me this because she knew I worked for the government. I told her I just counted owls. I told Earl this and he chuckled.

"It's true, they've been seeding clouds out here since the seventies," said Earl. "But that's not really planting a storm, that's just slipping a cloud a roofie."

We pulled off the highway and onto an unnamed, unpaved, and unremarkable road that intersected with many others just like it along the way. We drove straight into the orange sand of the desert. The farther we drove out into the desert, the thicker the tension seemed to grow between us. Mile after mile we drove, him grinning against the desert grit ahead of us, me, wishing I knew how to drive manual. I was usually a fairly good judge of character but if he did try to pull anything on me I'd be shit out of luck for stabbing the only one of us who knew how to drive us the hell out of the desert.

Earl told me that about this time last year he learned he could sew the seeds of a storm. He told me he could do this because he watched the water. Over there, he said pointing out the driver's side window into a clear patch of sky. He said just keep looking.

I fixed my eyes intensely to the spot, well aware that he now lay fully outside of my peripheral vision. My pocketknife felt bulky and awkward against my leg through the fabric of my jeans. Maybe I'd survive, I thought. Maybe a Forest Service surveyor like me would drive by and pick me up before I died of thirst, starvation, or exposure.

Earl pretended not to notice the gears turning in my head. Instead he told me to keep watching and soon I'd start seeing.

He eased the pick-up to a stop alongside a stretch of boulders that looked like cannon balls. I could tell they were from a younger rock formation because they sat gray and cracked against the orange sand and just above them stood a ridge their own color. They'd shaken loose and fallen a couple thousand years into the past in just a matter of meters.

Earl turned off the engine and slid out of the cab. I followed suit, eyes fixed on the sky, dry hot wind biting at them. Oddly enough, a soft coating of clouds had gathered across it, lightly dusting the stratosphere. Being out in the open I relaxed. Earl didn't feel as imminent standing a respectable distance from me as I continued to watch the sky. The desert didn't feel so deadly.

"That up there," said Earl, "that's water meeting herself. Keep on watching."

He climbed atop a cannon ball-shaped boulder, dislodged from time and heaped upon its predecessor. He cracked a beer and offered it to me. I hardly noticed. A spotted owl swooped overhead, between the sky and me and eased herself down into the brush sprouting up on the ridge overhead. Graceful and perfect. I wondered if I'd have even noticed had I not spent the last three months training my eyes to see her. How many owls had I missed in my whole life? Desert life is subtle; desert life takes little and leaves even less behind. Desert life hides from each other. Yet, there she was. My heart lurched from its seat and dropped a foot into my stomach. I felt the boulders before me roll through my bones and crush my heart.

"What the fuck is going on?" I demanded.

"You've become the desert, you're dropping a seed."

He nudged my arm with the warm

beer can and I accepted. I broke gaze with that special spot of sky where water met herself and decided to stick around. By that time, a full cloud had formed. I sat down on the boulder beside Earl. His blue eyes twinkled in the sunlight. Salty water droplets beaded at his brow, sliding down the creases that marked his years in the expressions that had passed across his face.

That night it poured.

When Water Meets Herself by Rebecca Little
was originally published in
Torches n' Pitchforks Online Literary Journal.
Reprinted here with permission.
To find out more about Torches n' Pitchforks,
please visit them online at
http://www.torchesnpitchforks.com.

LET INDIE ARTIST PRESS HELP
YOU PUBLISH YOUR NOVEL!

Are you a writer? Looking to become an author through the art of publishing your novel, poetry, how-to book or memoir? If you've written a book and would like to learn more about the immense benefits of self-publishing, we'd like to help.

Indie Artist Press is the first non-publisher publisher dedicated to helping YOU succeed.

What makes us different from a vanity press?

A vanity press charges you for the privilege of printing/publishing your book. They do not:

- Edit your book for grammar or typing errors
- Edit your book for continuity
- Edit your book for characterization or plot
- Care, one way or another, whether you succeed
- Care, one way or another, whether they are selling quality literature

They don't care because you have already paid them! But that won't stop them from keeping 80% or more of each retail sale price, paying you only about 20% in royalties. You've paid the costs of publishing, and they keep the lion's share of your money. Sound fair? We didn't think so, either.

Indie Artist Press will charge you less and do so much more! *We can* :

- Edit your book for grammar, typing errors
- Edit your book for continuity, characterization, plot
- Design a customized book cover
- Format your manuscript for print and digital distribution
- Help you set up your payee account through your bookseller of choice so that 100% of the proceeds of your book are delivered directly to you!
- Help you design your website and social marketing venues
- Create promotional materials to help you market your book
- Work with you to create a payment plan that fits your needs and overall goals for success

We have several plans to choose from, all for far less than you can expect to pay to a vanity press, or even a "traditional" publisher. When you "sell" your book to a publisher through a publishing contract, you are giving away up to 90% or more of your money for the rest of your life, and sometimes even longer. (When a publishing house contracts your book for the life of the copyright, that's your natural life, plus another 70 years.)

Why not invest in your own product by securing top-of-the-line editing and other services and then keep 100% of your earnings for the next several decades and beyond?

Please visit indieartistpress.com to learn more about how we can help you publish your first book, or your next book, with affordable, professional services.

Indie Artist Press

SAVE 25% on Editing Services from

Indie Artist Press!

Mention this coupon when you submit your manuscript for review and, if your manuscript is accepted into our program, we'll slash the cost of your editing package* by 25%.

*Does not include Mind, Body or Spirit Packages and may be redeemed only on The Whole She-bang or higher level packages. The purchase of an editing package does not guarantee publication with IAP and all manuscripts must be fully vetted prior to publication. If your manuscript has been selected for publication, you will be offered a contract with IAP and all terms of that contract apply. To view the terms of our contracts, please visit **www.indieartistpress.com**.

Beckyjean G. Cooke
Written Tapestries
A Collection of Poetry
We all lie exposed to the world
or ourselves. It can be both
exhilarating and terrifying.
We bare all for hope, for the
chance of finding Soul.

Please, enjoy a sneak peek at
Loving the Heartland by *Marjorie Jones*
*#3 Best Seller for Lesbian Romance/Lesbian Fiction
on Amazon.com (US and UK Markets!)*

"A wonderful tale of family, honor and love. I would recommend this book to everyone that I know." **Five Stars** *Amazon Reader Review*

"Heartstopping... a story I could read again... You won't be disappointed with this." **Five Stars** *Amazon Reader Review*

"Please don't miss this; Highly recommend!" **Five Stars** *Amazon Reader Review*

AvailableNOW!
*Kindle Unlimited
& Kindle Owners Lending Library
Print Version is Prime Eligible*

Bright lights. Big City.

Traffic inched over Las Vegas Boulevard. The slice of Nevada desert glowed bright as day even though the neon-green display on Michelle's dashboard clock read eleven-thirty p.m. Hundreds of tourists meandered along the streets, mingling through the shops and casinos as if time meant nothing. And to them, perhaps it didn't. But to Michelle? Time meant money and she had only fifteen minutes to meet her friend, Lacey Williams, before Lacey had to go back to work.

The great Frank Sinatra, whose indelible imprint still marked Sin City, once said that New York was the city that never slept. Truth be told, Las Vegas ranked a close second in that regard. When she finished her meeting with Lacey, she'd need to race home and put the finishing touches on a project she'd been working on for Brianna Kincaid, one of her biggest clients. She owned the hottest lesbian club in town and was planning to launch a new gay club right next door in the next three weeks.

A gap opened in the lane to her right and she slid her tiny convertible sports car into the slot. Lacey's casino stood on the next corner. She just might make her meeting in time, after all.

Several young men, not one looking older than twenty-two, crossed the street in front of her. The apparent leader of the pack turned in her direction and opened his muscled arms wide, showing off a hard chest beneath a casually-opened dress shirt. "Hey baby," he shouted over her windshield. "You wanna party?"

Oh, yeah. He's toasted.

She gave him her very best I'm-a-local-get-out-of-my-way grin and waited for them to finish crossing the street before she stomped the gas pedal and made for the corner. If they only knew, she thought, shaking her head at the concept that men were all interested in the same thing.

She slipped into the valet parking lane in front of a huge hotel resort and waited for George, the attendant, to claim her car. Gathering her purse, tablet and digital camera, she climbed from behind the wheel.

George, an older guy with a ring of silver hair and a face that would be at home in any mob movie rushed in to take her seat. "Hey there, girly. You lookin' for Lacey?"

"Yup. Is she in her regular pit?" Michelle handed him a ten dollar bill then took the claim ticket.

"Not tonight. She's been workin' the Blackjack table. Pit three, I think."

"Thanks, Georgie. I won't be too long."

More bright lights met her in the lobby. Bells and sirens, laughter and the artificial clank of coins hitting metal trays deafened her as soon as she entered the casino. A slight ache developed in the back of her head.

She dodged a group of elderly ladies making a bee-line for the nickel slots and made her way to the Blackjack tables.

Waving to several friends along the way, she skirted the last pit and found a table in the tiny bar on the far side. Less than a minute later, Lacey plopped into the seat across from her.

"I swear, Mike," Lacey declared, using the nickname she'd given to Michelle at their first meeting, "I'm going to have to buy new feet before I ever save enough for next year's tuition." Lacey leaned forward in her chair and rubbed her ankles. They were very nice looking ankles.

Michelle forced her attention back to Lacey's face and smiled. She was a pretty girl, with large, green eyes; perfect skin. Her looks were classic and would fit very well in her chosen career as a television journalist. She was majoring in broadcasting and communication at UNLV. Any station or network would be lucky to have her, someday. "Beats the hell out of working a register or turning burgers for minimum wage, right?"

"True." Lacey leaned back and tugged at the strapless top of her cocktail uniform. The sexy black number barely concealed her ample breasts. "I'll make it quick," she continued. "I know you're busy. I took an early out. Let me run and change, and I'll be right back." Lacey climbed out of the chair and headed toward the employee locker room.

Not for the first time, Michelle admired her friend's retreat. Naturally blonde and sexy, she exuded confidence and grace. Despite her complaints of sore feet, she moved with an assured sensuality that was purely femme. Michelle was femme, too, but unlike Lacey, these days she could barely walk in low-heeled pumps much less maneuver a casino floor in a strapless mini-dress and four-inch spikes.

She admired Lacey for doing what she had to do in order to finish her education. There was a time when Michelle had done the same thing. Fifteen years earlier, Michelle had been the girl schlepping drinks, hoping for tips big enough to help her make rent. She'd worn the skimpy outfits, put up with men pawing her every chance they got, and sucking up the revulsion. She'd even worn the heels.

Not anymore.

Now she owned her own public relations firm in a city bent on its own self-image. Life was good. With more than a dozen employees, she managed a busy and successful virtual office and produced mobile, internet and print advertising for some of the biggest resorts in a sprawling oasis of decadence and opulence.

Michelle ordered a Long Island Iced Tea and made sure to tip the waitress very well. By the time it arrived, Lacey, looking more comfortable in blue jeans, a UNLV sweatshirt and sensible tennis shoes, reclaimed her seat.

Lacey smiled and waved at the bartender.

"So," Michelle began. "What's so important that it couldn't wait until morning?"

Lacey made an attempt to look coy and relaxed and then, true to her transparent nature, gave up. She preened in her chair and beamed a smile full of even, white teeth. "Okay, I talked to my sister and she thinks it's a great idea. She wants the complete package. Photos. Video. Everything. Oh, and a website. The works."

Michelle choked on her drink. "Are you serious? Miss-I-Have-No-Idea-What-Century-I-Live-In wants a website?"

Lacey's hands fell to her lap and she toyed with her fingernails.

"I knew it. You're lying," Michelle groaned.

"Not entirely. Casey loved the idea and thinks it could only help the ranch!"

"Point in fact. Casey is your brother, not your sister."

"Kendra is practically a man, Michelle; it's not always easy to tell them apart."

Michelle kicked Lacey under the table and gave her a look. They had often discussed how bizarre her family was – five kids, only two girls, and both of them lesbians. "But Casey isn't in charge, is he? Last time we discussed this project, Kendra had no love for anything less than a hundred years old. She wanted no part of your little plan to save the family homestead."

"That's because she's a moron. C'mon, Michelle. Say you'll do it! Please? The ranch has been in our family for over a century – five generations. Once you get there and show Kendra what a great tool the Internet really is, and how powerful the images you're going to produce are, I'm sure she'll come around."

"And in the meantime, I'm doing what? Scurrying about underfoot and making her life miserable? No, thank you."

"You couldn't make anyone miserable if you tried."

Michelle snorted and took another sip of her drink. "Tell that to my mother."

Lacey rolled her eyes and flopped back in her chair. "So, you'll do it?"

Michelle paused, drilling Lacey with a double-barreled stare. Finally, she sighed. "Yes, I'll do it. But I swear, one of these days, I'm going to learn how to pronounce the word, 'No.'"

"How soon can you leave for Utah?"

"Day after tomorrow, I guess. I only have one project on the wire right now and I'll be finished with the pics tonight. I can turn over the roll-out to Miranda and drive out to your folks place on Wednesday. The rest of the staff manage their own projects and can keep me in the loop on Skype."

"This is going to work. I just know it."

"Don't get your hopes up, Lacey." Michelle's expression fell. "The government has an uncanny way of looking out for itself. If Kendra isn't willing to play their game, the developers might very well take that land for their resort and she'll have to find somewhere else to raise her cows. Money talks, you know?"

"Yeah, I know. But I'm an eternal optimist, remember? The lease doesn't expire for another year, so we have time. We have plenty of time."

Michelle harbored more than a few doubts about this particular project. The first time Lacey had asked her about it, almost six months ago, she had given Michelle all the details surrounding her elder sister. Born a century too late, Kendra Williams seemed the epitome of an old west loner. According to Lacey, she'd raised all four of her siblings, most of them male, alone after her mother and father had been killed in a private plane crash before Lacey had been eight years old. Her descriptions of her sister-turned-guardian fit more readily into the mold of an old western movie than that of a modern ranch owner. She still rode the fences and shoed her own horses. Lacey hadn't watched cable TV while growing up, played video games or anything else a typical American teen should have experienced at the turn of the new century. Of course, Kendra would have been miserable had she actually been born in the old west. Even Calamity Jane had been forced to wear a dress much of the time. Michelle had a feeling that Kendra never would.

Still, Michelle knew how to promote and advertise a business. If she could convince an entire generation of Americans that Las Vegas was the perfect family destination, she could convince anyone of anything. If Kendra remained lost in her dreams of the past, the future would come in and rip out all of those roots she'd so painstakingly protected.

And Michelle's job would be that much harder.

"Screw you, Mac!"

Kendra Williams winced at her brother's lack of respect. Then she slapped him on the back of his head and pulled him away from the Randall County Sheriff, Mac Lawrence. "Settle down, Case. Mind your manners."

"He can't keep us out of that meeting, Kennie."

Kendra dragged her head-strong, younger brother through the lobby of the county courthouse by the breast of his leather biker jacket; past the statue of the coal miner and portraits of twenty Miss Randall Counties, including his twin sister, Lacey. Kendra tossed him toward the double glass doors facing Main Street. "Casey, there is a time and a place for everything, and right now is not the time or the place for your temper. I hate this as much as you do, but we have to live here with these people and pissing of the sheriff isn't going to help our cause."

"That old windbag can't keep us out of a

public meeting that has to do with our land!"

"Get your ass in the truck and wait for me."

Casey stood his ground, both an annoying and admirable trait shared by all of the Williams clan. Kendra put her hands low on her hips and released a calming breath. In addition to the stubborn streak, Casey had a knack for dragging trouble with him wherever he went. If he'd just shut up and get in the truck, Kendra could figure out a way to get into that meeting. After a brief moment that felt like ten minutes, Casey turned and strode out of the building.

"He's a pistol, Kennie." The sheriff slid next to her and put his hands in his trouser pockets, his head moving from side to side in forlorn desperation.

Kendra ran a hand through her hair and grimaced, keeping her focus straight ahead. "That he is, Mac. I just wish he'd quit misfiring." She turned to face her old friend. "So, you gonna let me in that meeting?"

"Now, Kendra. The commissioners aren't going to side with some out-of-town developers over you. You know that. What good will it do for you to sit in on a zoning meeting when the request will be denied, anyway? You really didn't even need to come into town for this."

"I lost another forty head last week."

As soon as the words left her mouth, the air in the room changed. Mere tension moved aside for the stirrings of real trouble, sending a finger of electricity over the short hairs on the nape of her neck. Silence stretched for more than a moment before Mac answered.

"Shot?"

"We think so."

Mac released a slow breath and crossed his arms over his chest. Kendra finally looked over at him. She'd known Mac for thirty years. They went to grade school together and then dated briefly in high school before Kendra had grown the balls to tell him she was a lesbian. Not that he'd been much surprised, as she'd found out when he'd breathed a sigh of relief that she wasn't really going to keep faking it. He was the kind of guy who would probably have married her rather than confront her about it.

The high school gym where they'd had this very serious conversation sat about four blocks east of where they stood at that moment. The same school that Mac's daughter, Lenise, attended with Kendra's youngest brother, Brad. Brad and Lenise had been dating for two years and recently attended the junior prom together.

That's what small towns were made of. Families. Generations. Stories.

The Williams' had worked the land and raised beef on a four-hundred acre spread at the Eastern edge of the county for a hundred years. Randall County took its name from her great-grandfather, Colonel John Randall, whose daughter had married a Williams and founded the Williams Cattle Company. The town hall was named after her uncle, one of the first county commissioners.

No way was a group of dandies from New York City, of all places, going to come in here and take what wasn't theirs.

Find Loving the Heartland in print and Kindle formats at Indie Artist Press:
http://www.indieartistpress.com.